BAD KITTY

Takes the Test

NICK BRUEL

A NEAL PORTER BOOK
ROARING BROOK PRESS
NEW YORK

To Aurora

Copyright © 2017 by Nick Bruel

A Neal Porter Book

Published by Roaring Brook Press

Roaring Brook Press is a division of Holtzbrinck Publishing Holdings Limited Partnership

175 Fifth Avenue, New York, New York 10010

mackids.com

Library of Congress Cataloging-in-Publication Data

Names: Bruel, Nick, author, illustrator.

Title: Bad Kitty takes the test / Nick Bruel.

Description: First edition. | New York : Roaring Brook Press, 2017. | Series:
Bad Kitty | "A Neal Porter Book" | Summary: Because of a recent string of
embarrassing behavior, Kitty's cat license has been revoked and she must
take a test to get it back so she can still be a cat.

Identifiers: LCCN 2016027113 | ISBN 9781626725898 (hardback)

Subjects: | CYAC: Cats–Fiction. | Behavior–Fiction. | Test
anxiety–Fiction. | Humorous stories. | BISAC: JUVENILE FICTION / Animals
/ Cats. | JUVENILE FICTION / Humorous Stories.

Classification: LCC PZ7.B82832 Baok 2017 | DDC [E]–dc23

LC record available at https://lccn.loc.gov/2016027113

Our books may be purchased in bulk for promotional, educational, or business use. Please
contact your local bookseller or the Macmillan Corporate and Premium Sales Department
at (800) 221-7945 ext. 5442 or by e-mail at MacmillanSpecialMarkets@macmillan.com.

First edition 2017

Printed in the United States of America by LSC Communications US, LLC
(Lakeside Classic), Harrrisonburg, Virginia

1 3 5 7 9 10 8 6 4 2

• CONTENTS •

•CHAPTER ONE•

BAD KITTY DOES NOT LIKE BIRDS

Kitty loves birds.

She loves how they flit.
She loves how they flap.
She loves how they flutter.
She loves how they poo.

When Kitty sees birds,
she wants to play with them.

She really, really, REALLY
wants to play with them.

The birds also want to play with Kitty.
They want to play hide-and-seek.

The birds are very good at hiding.
They're hiding in the tree.

But Kitty sees them!

Kitty is very good at seeking.
And she's very good at climbing.

Kitty finds the birds again!
Kitty is very good at this game.

So are the birds.

The birds keep hiding
higher and higher.

Kitty keeps climbing
higher and higher.

Soon, the birds are at the top of the tree. There is no tree left.

Now Kitty wants to play another game with her new friends: TAG!

But the birds don't want to play that game.
Too bad.

Now Kitty has no one to play with.

Uh-oh.

Oh, good! The birds have come back to play with Kitty and help her down from the tree.

But Kitty does not want their help. She just wants to go home.

WHACK
WHACK
WHACK
WHACK
WHACK
WHACK
WHACK
WHACK
WHACK

THUD!

Kitty does not
like birds.

•CHAPTER TWO•
THE NEXT DAY

Good morning, Kitty.

The mail's here, and it looks like you have a certified letter from the Society of Cat Aptitude Management. I've never heard of them. Have you?

Uh-oh. This doesn't look good.

It looks like they know about your run-in with those birds yesterday. Apparently it's considered the most recent instance in a long line of "shameful un-catlike embarrassments." Others include the time you . . .

woke up suddenly and
fell behind the
sofa,

got stuck in the
venetian blinds,

were frightened by
a spider, which
turned out to be
a ball of lint,

22

tried to jump
on the desk
but landed
in the
plants,

allowed the baby
to dress you up
for Halloween,

and let the
dog sit on
you while
you were
sleeping.

So apparently because of this recent string of embarrassing behavior, your cat license has been REVOKED.

I didn't even know there was such a thing.

The letter goes on.

In order to renew your cat license, you have to take a special course on being a cat, followed by a TEST. This all happens tomorrow!

A test? Well, Kitty, a test is a process you go through to make sure you understand everything you've learned.

Now pay attention, Kitty. Here's the important part. If you PASS the test, then you'll get your license back.

I didn't even know you had one to begin with.

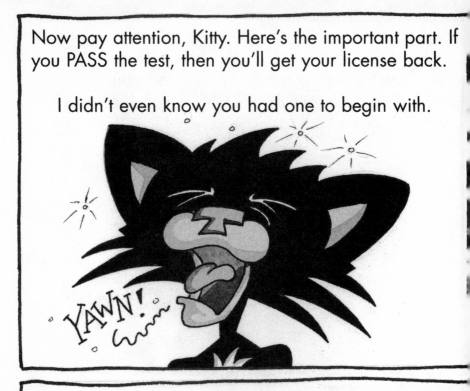

But if you DON'T pass the test . . . well . . . according to this letter, then you won't get your license and then apparently you won't . . . gosh . . . you won't be allowed to be a cat anymore!

Kitty, I don't make the rules. All I know is that you need to take this test tomorrow whether you like it or not. I have the address. I'll bring you there in the morning.

ARE YOU INSANE?

And will you please stop writing on the walls?! I've had to call the painters 14 times this month.

Kitty?! **KITTY!!!**
Sigh.

* I HAVE to pass this test! I NEED to pass this test. If I don't pass this test, then I won't be a cat. I don't know what I'd be. Maybe I'd be a walrus. I don't want to be a walrus. I'm sensitive to cold weather. I haven't slept in three days.

33

41

- A cat is an animal.

- A giant squid is also an animal. It has tentacles.

- Cats do not have tentacles, therefore they are rarely mistaken for giant squids.

- Other animals that are not cats are squirrels, giraffes, lobsters, and porcupines.

- Cats typically have four legs. If a cat has less than four legs or more than four legs, then something is wrong and medical attention may be required.

- In 1963, the French sent the first cat into space, a black-and-white Parisian street cat named Félicette who traveled 100 miles above the Earth in a capsule before descending safely back to the ground by parachute.

- "Cat" in Vietnamese is *con mèo*.

- The World Health Organization estimates that approximately 400,000 people are bitten by cats in the United States every year. No one has died from their injuries.

- "Cat" in Swahili is *paka*.

• Legend has it that Sir Isaac Newton, the scientist and mathematician who discovered gravitational mechanics and created calculus, also invented the cat flap on doors because he was tired of constantly getting up from his experiments to let his cat, Spithead, in and out of his study.

• That's right . . . Sir Isaac Newton named his cat Spithead.

• "Cat" in Icelandic is *köttur*.

• "Cat" spelled backward is "tac," which are the first three letters in the word "taco," which is a delicious food that cats will sometimes eat when dropped on the floor.

• In the early 1960s, the CIA launched Operation Acoustic Kitty, an actual plan to use cats as spies. Cats would be trained to eavesdrop on Russian conversations. They would be released nearby with microphones implanted in their ears, transmitters attached to their collars, and antennae tied to their tails. The first cat agent was deployed and then run over by a taxi moments later. Twenty million dollars was spent on the program that was terminated shortly thereafter.

• Spithead.

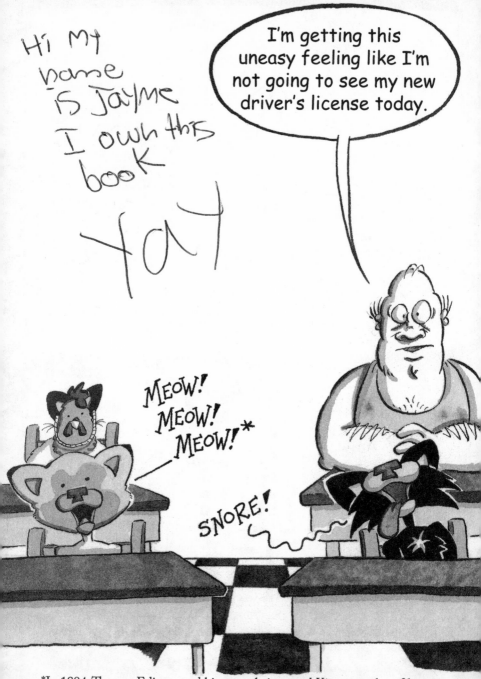

*In 1894, Thomas Edison used his recently invented Kinetograph to film two cats boxing. It is considered to be the very first cat video. I hope THAT'S on the test!

The owners of the #3 pencil factory have contacted us. They would like to propose an alliance and join us in our mission.

THOSE PIGS CAN GO TO BLAZES!

We don't need them! We control the pencils that control the tests! Soon we will control the minds and intellect of the entire WORLD . . . beginning with the CATS!

MWAH-HAH-HAH-HAH-HAH-HAH-HAH-BUK-HAH-HAH-HAH-HAH-BUK-BUK-HAH-HAH-BUK-BUK-HAH!

* MAKE IT STOP! I just want to take the %#@$§• test! I don't want to take tests that will prepare me for the next test that will prepare me for the next test that will . . .

* How many tests is it really?

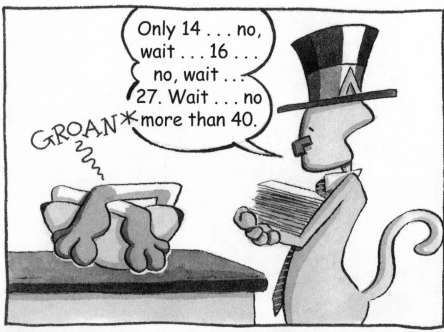

* Groan

Listen, Chatty. You're just nervous is all, which is understandable. Try not to worry so much. Worrying is not going to help you take this test.

I'll make a deal with you. If you pass the final test, I'll buy you a chocolate tuna milkshake in celebration. And if you don't pass, I'll still buy you one to make you feel better. Deal?

MEOW*

*That sounds simultaneously disgusting and exquisite.

71

* Ahem! Can I help you?

*Are you looking for something? Did you lose your pencil? Do you need more paper?

* Are you aware that psychologists recommend clear personal boundaries be set between two individuals in order to ensure an environment wherein their relationship can remain mutually respectful and supportive? And I can smell what you had for lunch.

* OVER HERE! LOOK AT ME! I NEED ATTENTION AND ASSISTANCE RIGHT AWAY!

* "I would prefer even to fail with honor than win by cheating." —Sophocles.

* Actually, the average cat has around 16 separate vocalizations with which they can communicate. This does not include body language like tail twitching or the roars that large cats commonly use . . .

* Just tell me what you want me to say, and I'll say it.

This proves that _____.

A) the test is fair
B) chickens are smarter than cats
C) this is definitely, DEFINITELY not, not, NOT part of an overall scheme to prove to the world that chickens are smarter than cats and always have been so that chickens will eventually be kept as pets inside nice, warm houses while cats will be served at dinnertime on a bed of rice next to potatoes and green beans
D) someday chickens will rule the world

Answer: A

Extra credit.

* I can't do it!

* What if I fail?!

* But everyone will think I'm a dummy.

* I will. I'll feel like a dummy.

* I'll try.

* That's not an egg, is it?

MEOW MEOW MEOW MEOW MEOW MEOW MEOW MEOW MEOW MEOW MEOW MEOW MEOW MEOW MEOW MEOW MEOW MEOW MEOW MEOW MEOW MEOW MEOW MEOW MEOW MEOW MEOW MEOW MEOW MEOW MEOW*

* Approximately 1.1 trillion eggs are consumed worldwide each year, China being the largest producer. Roughly half of all eggs produced are white, and the other half are brown. The color of the egg depends largely on the color of the earlobe of the chicken that laid it: white earlobe, white egg—red earlobe, brown egg. Egg shells are composed primarily of calcium carbonate, which is also the main ingredient in some antacids, but I don't recommend chewing on egg shells if you have an upset stomach. The membrane inside the shell is semipermeable, meaning that it allows water and oxygen inside the egg while keeping dust and other debris out. The white of an egg is also called the albumin after the primary protein that inhabits it. If an egg white looks cloudy, that actually means that the egg is very fresh. The color of the egg yolk depends greatly on the diet of the chicken that laid it: the more yellow or orange pigments in the food, the more brightly colored the yolk. A monotreme is a mammal that lays an egg, and there are only five known species in the world, the platypus and four species of echidna. The largest eggs come from ostriches, which can weigh as much as 5 pounds, and the smallest eggs come from vervain hummingbirds, which weigh only a fraction of an ounce. And lastly, a person who is considered to be intellectually gifted is often referred to as an egghead. I've been called an egghead. I wasn't insulted.

* Shall I tell you everything I know about dishwashers?

HEH-
HEH-
—HEH!

•CHAPTER SEVEN•
THE NEXT, NEXT, NEXT DAY

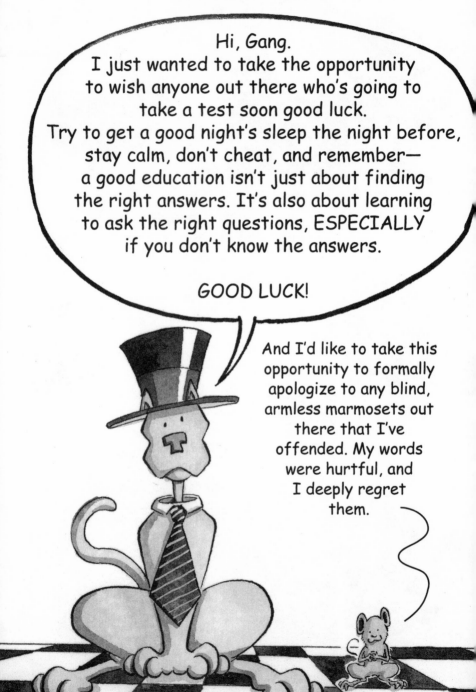